Joshua Hatton

Daphnis the Unfaithful

A Poetic Romance

Joshua Hatton

Daphnis the Unfaithful
A Poetic Romance

ISBN/EAN: 9783337348700

Printed in Europe, USA, Canada, Australia, Japan

Cover: Foto ©Andreas Hilbeck / pixelio.de

More available books at **www.hansebooks.com**

DAPHNIS THE UNFAITHFUL.

(A POETIC ROMANCE.)

BY

Guy Roslyn, a minor.

" Of Hony and of Gaule in love there is store;
The Honye is much, but the Gaule is more."

LONDON:
JOHN CAMDEN HOTTEN, 74 & 75, PICCADILLY.
1870.

TO

BARRY SULLIVAN,

This Poem is Dedicated

BY THE AUTHOR.

DAPHNIS.

Now Fancy smile ! and quietly I'll doze
Within thy airy bow'rs of calm repose :
O spread thy purple wings that I may fly
On saffron rays of sunset 'bout the sky !
To where yon clouds embrace the sun's last gleams,
There let me bathe in soul-reviving dreams.
Or we will tarry in new-budding dales,
And I will hearken to thy curious tales
Of Fairyland—all mixed with wondrous sights
Of things unsearchable and cloudy flights
To far-off stars, where easy 'tis to trace
Our tiny earth and moon roll on in space.

Have I not basked with thee in summer's sky?
And left the city's crazy din to lie
On daisy lawns, whilst thou did'st weirdly sing
And all about delicious odours bring?
Yea, and I've seen all beauties with a name—
The sweetest nymphs, and fairies' moonlight game.

From Hades to Olympus overhead,
From earth to sky and sky to sea we fled.
Old Neptune's coral palaces concealed
Beneath the murmuring ocean, stood revealed.
We've walked with Oceanides below,
'Mid sapphires and the diamond's crystal glow,
And strayed through caves of pearly sea-shells made,
Where fishes in a merry gambol played.
Or when the waves in anger sought to fly
From out their bounds unto the cloudy sky,
We sped in safety on the sea-bird's back,
And followed in the howling tempest's track.
Soon as the waves in peace their offerings bore
Unto the bosom of the shingly shore,

Wrapt in the fine serenity of night
We danced with Nereus' many daughters bright.

But Fancy, if we list to Reason stern,
Then 'tis mere nothingness ; for he doth turn
Our musing to vanity—nought save sound
Hears he in purling rills that joyful bound
'Bout Flora's flow'ry halls : no plaintive song
That bids us ponder as we pass along.

At dead of night, the ever tranquil time,
When drowsy humankind long hours sublime
In slumbers all the sweetest moments pass ;
When darting by the twinkling starry mass
Pale-visag'd Hecate hurls along the air,
With lightning's magic speed and sudden glare,
The fire-wing'd meteor, mysterious sign
For wicked ouphs and imps to howl and whine—
Signal for ghosts' and witches' crazy flight
That haunt the frightened mind of man by night.
Fancy ! then all my soul has clung to thee,
And vanished from this noisy world to see

The shadowy past : Apollo tread the plains
Of this our earth to charm with mellow strains
The rocks and listening trees, and bring around
In tameness birds and beasts, lured by the sound.
Thou showed'st me Hector in the midst of war,
Dealing out death on all sides, and I saw
Achilles from his chariot destroy
Great warriors, the pride and boast of Troy.
I sighed with thee e'en for Prometheus' woes,
Poor Niobe's despair—Ixion's throes.

O come unto me now ! for I would fain
Behold the wonders of the past again.
In sleepy wakefulness around me bring
The enchanting scene : let maidens sing
Sweet roundelays upon their native hills,
Bestrewn with spicy herbs and daffodils.
Close all my senses to th' incessant din
About me, and now soothingly begin :
In glens Sicilian new freshness pour,
Raise up again the immortals, and store

With nymphs and dryads all the woody ways,
And let them dance to old Pan's jolly lays.
Let shepherds tune their pipes upon the side
Of Etna, and her giant host that hide
Their heads eternally 'neath snowy shrouds,
That stretch unto the sky, and kiss the clouds.

 Of Daphnis, shepherd of Sicilian land,
Whose joys to woes by Venus' artful hand
Were turned, and in the early walk of life
Each pleasing duty sacrificed to strife,
(Poor shepherd !) faltering will I relate,
Until the darkest shades of night await
On flitting rays of setting sun to cease
Their frolic with the streams and sighing trees.
Here on this mossy bank, while round me play
Wind-wafted leaves, I'll listen to the lay
Of Zephyr-kiss'd reeds, sweetly-piping birds,
And shape them at thy will, O muse ! to words.
Here will I, where my story was begun,
Linger many evenings, till flowers have done

To bloom 'pon earth—honeysuckle, lilies too,
And modest hyacinths with bells of blue ;
Till everyone shall dwindle, droop, and die,
And graceful grass, low, withering shall lie ;
Fall'n 'neath scythe, with parting breath so sweet,—
No more Apollo's morning fire to greet.

    Yet while ye are, O help me to unfold
My story ! now while meadows sleep in gold,
Ay now, while through the dingles, brakes, and dells
Are wafted sounds of Nature's many bells.
Now, while the linnet, on the tender spray
Of blooming hawthorn, sings her thrilling lay.
Till the horizon shall no longer glow,
And hazy mists about dank pastures grow.
Till bats and creatures of the night arise,
And ghost-like flit about the dark'ning skies.

———

    Boreas, once a day, with icy chains
Encircled all the earth, and blooming plains

Lost all their verdure—every running brook
Was stilled by his keen breath, and every nook
In gloominess was lost—cold, sad, and drear.
Imprisoned thus the earth rolled many a year ;
Till Zephyrus denied his brother's sway,
And with th' aid of Flora drove the god away.
The chains of ice were melted, earth made free,
Fair flowers re-appeared, and every tree
Regained its beauty, as returning spring
Taught brooks to bubble, and the birds to sing.
The power was then divided by the gods,
But in that favoured isle where Etna nods
Perpetual spring was granted ; since that time
No cruel blasts have dared to chill the clime.
Though seasons roll, and winter takes the place
Of mellow autumn, yet to Sicily's race
Winter's a spring, for fanned across the seas
For ever comes the genial summer breeze :
And even as the hottest days prevail
The heat is tempered by a cooling gale.

Now morning, hastening through the clouds of
    night,
Comes on apace : enrobed in feathery light
Aurora leaves her downy couch to rise,
And draws her golden wand across the skies.
Down from her car the goddess of the dawn
Sprinkles her rosy favours o'er the lawn.
Rejoicing fields with glistening dewdrops shine,
And on the weeping hills young lambkins whine.
The wakening meadows, too, with music ring
And new-born freshness is with everything.

Amid the glow of early morning's hour,
A tender nymph, slow pacing, left her bower ;
Slowly she walks as in a troubled dream
With painful countenance—the tears stream
Adown her cheeks.   O it were piteous care
Should blight a pretty maiden, young and fair !
Ah Cupid! wanton boy, again thy freaks
Have hapless proved, but list ! the maiden speaks :

" Ah me ! nine times hath Helios sped
'Cross the sky, and nine nights o'erhead
Hath Luna thrown her darts to dight
The mountain tops in silver light,
Since my sweet little babe first breathed—
Since his frail tiny breast first heaved.
O precious fondling ! when I view
Its puny eyes of heavenly blue,
The father's face comes to my mind—
The face of Hermes so unkind !
My bower is now forsaken quite—
A place of tears from morn till night—
When he was by me all was gay—
His smile bade every care away.
In whispers gentle as a dove,
For me he vowed his constant love.
Each meeting, like young Iris' ray,
Scarce dawned, ere it did fade away.
So quick the time when lovers meet,
And pleasures every moment greet.

When he was nigh each view seemed lush
With loveliness : the warbling thrush
Sang sweeter still, but when he left
To meet the gods I was bereft
Of peace.

        " For him I vainly seek,
My love is more than I can speak.
Ah me !' I asked that I might never
Die, but live like him for ever.
Oh bitter fate he left me then,
Nor will he come to me again
To ease my woe.   Oh fatal day !
Thus I must slowly pine away !

   " My sister nymphs, my child shall keep,
Attend upon his couch of sleep,
And lead him with a kindly hand
From day to day unto the Land
Of Life, where quickly Fate will show
His destined happiness or woe.

To death then will I turn my face,
And in the gloomy regions trace
My love, whose absence hurts me more
Than all the fear of Styx's shore."

Alas ! what dizzy phantoms haunt the mind !
What fears, and cares, and wondrous hopes we find ⁚
By nourishing, in secret, vain desires,
The nymph to immortality aspires.
　Heart-sick her solitary way she took,
Towards a violet bank beside a brook ;
And tarried there awhile, relief to find
To ease her heart—forgetfulness of mind.
She turned her watery eyes with dreamy look
To where a flower, peeping from its nook,
Bent down its head as some poor stricken maid,
And as she gazed the water flower said :

" Immortal stream that laughs at mortals' day,
O mountain-born ! how merry is thy way

Singing at all time an enchanting song
By sedgy banks, and fruitful dales among,
Where overhanging branches meet and kiss
Thy limpid face !   O give to me this bliss,
Grant me, O ever cheerful stream ! that I
May travel on with thee, and never die."

Then in reply the brook : " Vain flower, forbear,
For fade away thou must like clouds in air ;
I will cherish and revive thee ever,
But share my endless life thou canst not—never !"

As brooding o'er imaginary care,
A sound of merry laughter rends the air,
And soon a band of nymphs skip o'er the plain
In playful gait, with now and then a strain
Of some neglected song.   They ran to where
Their sister nymph sat wrapped in dire despair.
Each looking at the other as in fear,
They gather round mysteriously to hear

What cruelty had wronged the weeping maid,
And caused so soon her rosy cheeks to fade,
Then with many offerings to invoke
The anger of the gods.   But thus she spoke :
   " My friends and sisters dear, why do ye start ?
Has never pain bid your own glee depart ?
Made your own eyes their quickness to forget ?
And crave to shun their truest friends to fret ?
Has never once dismay within your mind
Sorrow and solitude together twined ?
My grief was but a silly thought that preyed
Upon my mind.   But since I need your aid,
I must a secret tell : nine days have gone
Since to me was given, ah well—a son !
His father is great Hermes ! who above
For ever moves in fields of purest love.
If ye do worship him grant what I ask,
Or if ye have a care for me the task
Is but a pleasure.   My friends, years many
O'er life's gay paths or by-ways fenny

With you I've roamed.　Say, what then should I fear
In asking you my infant boy to rear?
To treat him kindly, and from day to day,
And year to year, to smoothe his earthly way?
For then, whenever death calls me away
With faithful hearts around my boy may stay.
Tell out your willingness, and ye I'll trace
Unto his future home—a secret place.
A laurel grove it is, on all sides bound
With nodding trees that sway unto the ground.
On honey of mountain bees let him be fed:
On goat's milk, dainty fruit, and sweetest bread—
And may the gods send blessings on his head.
Call my boy Daphnis.　Sisters, be always kind
To this my child, and sure reward ye'll find
From his immortal sire, who gave him breath.
Fear to wrong him as ye fear your death,
For sure as in his veins runs heavenly blood,
Evil will come to evil, good to good."

　　Then every nymph in joy and wonder mixed

Her gazing eyes upon the maiden fixed.

" O proud," said one of them, " must be the heart,

Though heaven-born, of her who doth impart

Graces to charm a god supremely wise,

Whose name is glorious throughout the skies !

Let ours be the willingness to serve

The paramour of him who doth preserve

Our herds upon the hills from erring ways,

Unto him may we evermore give praise.

But do thou favoured sister let us see

The gracious child whose comfort is to be

Our future trust."

             The thankful mother smiles,

And of her woe the gentle group beguiles,

Then to the bower that she had left in grief

Leads on the blithesome band feigning relief.

  The infant reached, the maidens joy express

By kisses and by many a soft caress.

The mother takes her child, and on they roam

O'er budding pathways to the secret home.

The sky was clear, the woods bright colours wore,
And gently-rushing rills ran on to pour
Sweet freshness unto flowers, that rest the head
'Neath juicy herbs or on a mossy bed.
And as they altogether trip along
Thus praise they Hermes' name in shepherds' song :

> Hear us, O thou who sprung
> From Maia and the god
> Who in sky the stars hath hung !—
> Earth totters at his nod !
> The favoured trust of all Olympus' host,
> Hear us, O Hermes ! thou of gods the boast.

> On Caucasus by thee was bound
> Prometheus with massive chain ;
> Direful woe fast flittered round,
> His groans re-echoed o'er the plain.
> An eagle from his breast the reeking liver drew,
> And eagerly devoured it, as it for ever grew.

> Hear us, O thou who brought
> To happiness man's race !

By speech to utter love and thought
    And movements make with grace.
Bearer of the wingèd hat, and the snaky rod ;
Guardian of our bleating flocks, hear us, great god !

When thou gave Heaven's command,
    In space Ixion fell,
Fixed by each foot and hand
    To the wheel that roll'd o'er hell.
Thus did'st thou inflict the punishment of Jove
On one of many who against Him strove.

By thee, great god, are led
    To future bliss or woe
The shadows of the dead—
    To heaven or flames below.
Hear us, O thou by every mortal bless'd !
Heed us, O thou of every god the guest !

The strains in air are lost of this their song,
And now in silence they the walk prolong.

2

A forest entering o'er many ways—
Soon it is passed, and thankfully they gaze
Upon the valley sheltered by a grove,
Where Pan to win the love of Syrinx strove,
Who fled to Ladon, and by him was freed—
The river god transformed her to a reed.
Long mourned the god of shepherds for the maid,
And from the reed he made a pipe, and played
His weary soul to rest.   Echo's love he lost
Though Pithy's love he gained, but she was tossed
High from a rock by Him of winter's blast—
The jealous Boreas—thus Pan's love passed.
The journey now is o'er, the spot they gain,
Young Daphnis and the nymphs long to remain.

  Carefully they left him in the grove,
Earnestly the mother watched her love,
Gently they formed a flowery bed,
Softly they laid his little head,
Sublimely the babe bathed in repose,
Swiftly the day drew to a close.

PART II.

IN Sicily, where snowy mountains climb,
To cloudland everlastingly; where Time
Nigh pow'rless proves—for those huge piles still
    show
Their mighty forms as centuries come and go—
The gentle Daphnis learnt to sing, and play
Upon the pipe; here passed his life away.

    A garden for the gods in olden time
Was Sicily—a paradise sublime !
The hills were clad with forests; paths between
Ran in and out o'ergrown with branches green.
There silver rivers through the valleys flowed,
And meadows many-coloured flowers showed.
The bounteous soil its greatest riches gave,
Nor did it ever cultivation crave.

    In such a fruitful country Daphnis slept,
And through the sunny hours of boyhood crept—
That run with magic speed; for Time will cheat
Poor mortals when he sees their lives are sweet.

He makes the tardy hours and days to pass
Like momentary thoughts, until, alas !
The golden dream of childhood all is o'er,
'Tis then we prize it, but it comes no more.
    E'en as a budding rose foretells its hue,
His faculties unfolded, and he grew
In favour well.   A manly frame he bore,
Yet he was graceful as might be, and wore
The beauty of a maiden.   Not a swain
In all the land could sing so sweet a strain.
When he took part in any pastoral game
There was not one to rob him of his fame :
He could outrun the swiftest in the race.
Of all his mates he had the kindest face
And bravest heart.

                    A shepherd youth was he
Passing his days about the mountains free ;
Where, often as he played upon the flute,
Diana stopped the hunt and listened mute :

Charmed by the sounds her heavenly coursers
    stayed,
And hearkened to him as he careless played.
'Twas Pan who taught him soul-inspiring strains,
As they together roamed along the plains—
The merry Pan who with Apollo strove
For finest music in the realms above,
And set the heart of every god aflame,
Whilst great Apollo failed and fled in shame.
    But Daphnis gradually, sad to tell,
Into the depths of melancholy fell.
His passion gained new power from day to day,
And he pursued his solitary way
Alone : he cared not with his friends to walk
And shunned the hearing of their idle talk :
He only sought to converse with a train
Of unshaped thoughts that thronged his wayward
    brain.
    His labours done, each evening he went
Unto a grotto, and secluded spent

Many long hours in brooding o'er his care,
He'd fix his eyes on nothingness, and stare,
Like some deluded swain who loves a maid
To madness, and is all the while afraid
To tell her so.

          The secret cause of strife,
Was the remembrance of his earlier life—
The mystery surrounding childhood's days
When he reclined beneath a mother's gaze.
How strange ! his mother used to tell him tales
Of immortality ! of happy vales
Where virtuous mortals go to soon as Death
Has sealed their eyes and ta'en away their breath.
A place of gorgeous meads, of untold joys
Where pleasure waits on all, but never cloys ;
Where hoary age is not, and beauty keeps
Its youth and fulness, and for ever reaps
New grace that once attained can never fade.
How marvellous ! and yet 'twas thus she said.
Alas ! his mother long ago had trod

Grim death's mysterious way to find the god
She loved ! a mighty god ! his father too !
He dare not doubt it—or believe it true.

   'Twas summer time ; Daphnis had been all day
Tending his flocks upon the hilly way.
He needed rest, and stretched his limbs beside
A rivulet—his woolly flocks too hied
To seek a shelter from the sun's fierce heat.
Soothing repose he found ; he dipped his feet
Into the cooling water ; o'er his head
Umbrageous foliage a cover spread.
The nodding osier bent adown to look
At its own form reflected in the brook.
The gurgling rivulet with soft sounds fell
O'er mossy stones, and murmured in the dell
Far off, like music falling through the air.
The shepherd fell asleep.

                A naiad fair
Espied the boy as on the bank he slept,
And silently on tiptoe to him crept.

She kissed his cheeks, but fearing he might wake,
Soon disappeared through a neighbouring brake.

He did not ope his eyes till clouds grew grey,
And now he leaves his sheep till morning's ray,
For fast the red sun hastens down the sky,
And sunset time in all its pomp draws nigh.
He rambles slowly down 'mid woodland thick :
But see ! behold the naiad follows quick,
With anxious countenance and trembling heart,
And still unwilling from the boy to part.
He did not see her, for upon the ground
He fixed his steadfast eyes, nor looked around.
And thus he passed along, and thus the maid
Followed in cautious steps as half afraid.

Soon came he near unto his favourite grot,
Concealed by ivy boughs—a quiet spot.
Weary he entered there awhile to rest
And watch the purple sunset in the west.

Then paused the naiad : her palpitating heart
Beat hard, and bade her oftentimes depart.

Full of hesitation, she tarried there,
Throbbing 'tween flattering hope and dark despair,
Till Venus urged her on; then seeming bold
Unto the grotto straightway to unfold
Her love for him she went; the silence broke
And blushing to the startled shepherd spoke:
" O precious being !" he felt his bosom swell,
" What may this mean?" he asked. "O I will tell,"
She answered eagerly, " for many a day
I've seen thee wand'ring on thy homeward way,
And foll'wing I have watched thee enter here,
Where I have ended my pursuit in fear.
Then dismal have I turned me slowly back
Heart-sick across the steep and lonely track.'
Oh ! I adore thee, lad ; nay, let me stay,
Nor crush so soon my cherished hopes I pray.
Grant that I may a little time beguile
With thee ; until the rising moon doth smile,
Till her soft shadows glimmer through these trees—
Grant my request, and set my heart at ease :

For then may I, without a thought of fear,

Whisper my secret soul into thine ear.

And I will woo thee, boy, whilst others steep

Their drowsy senses in the arms of sleep.

Forgive these hasty words of mine, I pray,

My ardour leads my better sense astray.

I only know that by great Jove above

'Thou art the only human thing I love."

The naiad ceased, and low down hung her head,

While in reply the baffled shepherd said :

" O thou who art as beautiful as kind,

With thine own feelings thou hast entwined

My soul : about my path that dismal grew

Hope doth her pleasing promises renew.

'Tis marvellous strange ! I had a dream last night :

Methought descending in refulgent light

A naiad came in this same grot and spoke

Even as thou hast done ; then I awoke

Before I could enfold her in my arms.

But sure thou art the owner of the charms

That she possessed in filmy dream—the same
And yet thou art a stranger, and thy name
Is all unknown to me."

      " Helen," said she,
" Is the name I bear; thine is known to me."
 " For certain," he continued, " thou didst take
The name of Helen for thy beauty's sake.
To be thy suitor and all time to spend
In thy sight, till existence shall have end,
Would be felicity, indeed, too fair
To fall methinks to my unworthy share.
Ay, Helen, do thou linger with me here,
For pleasantness will reign if thou be near,
And unto thee my truest vows I'll pour,
Passions that my young heart ne'er felt before."
 In pretty prattle they the time beguile,
Her snowy arms encircling him the while.
A wreath she made of roses red and white
To deck his brows—he was enraptured quite,

And kissed her cheeks till they were all aglow,
Then wished they weren't that he might make them so.

Unto the grotto love-gods came unseen,
And gambolled 'twixt the waving rushes green.
They skipped about the love-bewildered mates,
And pelted at each other's curly pates
Newly-plucked fruit and posies.

All around
The grotto danced a stream with gushing sound.
Hiding her face with her long wavy hair,
She sat down by his side, and lingered there.
Too deeply of her artifice he drank,
And powerless in her caresses sank.
At length the naiad sighing thus began :

"Too soon methinks, O shepherd, thou art won ;
My Daphnis wilt thou always constant be ?
For ever true and faithful unto me ?
Now list unto a tale, and mark it well,
'Tis one that goatherds and our shepherds tell :

A maiden dwells in Jove's domains above

For truthfulness and never changing love.

'Tis Psyche, youngest daughter of a king,

Whose comeliness to Venus sent a sting

Of jealousy, and made her troubled mind

Her own tormentor.   Ease she could not find ;

And rage to gentle ways soon made her blind.

Venus to tricksy Cupid went straightway

To tell her grief, and bade him lead astray

The maid's true passions, and inspire her mind

To dote upon a man of brutish kind.

In mischief rife her son to Psyche went,

And swift his golden bow in haste he bent,

That carries burning lust to highest bowers—

E'en black-browed Pluto owns its wondrous powers.

The god of love in his endeavours stopped,

And to the ground the useless bow it dropped ;

For he himself who playful hurls his darts

To wound or heal young lovers' tender hearts,

Scarce saw the graceful maid than he did yearn

With love sincere for her, and in return
She liked the god.   He carried her unseen
In secret to a charming spot serene,
And every night in haste he hurried there
To meet her ; never was a happier pair.
But she had sisters who drove her to fright,
Persuading her that he who came by night
Was but a monster foul.   Fear o'er her crept,
Yet she was brave.   At night as Cupid slept
She lit her lamp to see him.   As it blazed
In rapturous transport she upon him gazed.
When she beheld him doubt gave way to glee,
So exquisite the sleeping god to see !
E'en as she thanked th' immortals all was well,
From off the moving lamp there cruel fell
A drop of burning oil upon his arm !
She saw it fall and trembled with alarm !
Suddenly from his slumbers he awoke,
And angrily unto the damsel spoke.
Scorned all her silly mistrust, left the bed,

Upbraided her, and turning wrathful fled.

Now sorrow seized upon her, taught her sighs,

And filled with woeful tears her pretty eyes.

Alas ! calamity her heart did rend

And Death she asked adversity to end :

But he was silent to her earnest cry,

Nor would he ever grant that she should die.

Dull mourning worked apace, and bade her throw

Herself into a stream thus ending woe.

But she could not, some unseen ruling power

Turned the rash deed and saved the fading flow'r.

'Twas timely done, for hope regained a place

Within her, and she soon began to trace

The peevish boy who left her so unkind,

Yet scarcely ever thinking she should find

Him more.   Psyche unknowing where she went

Her giddy steps to Venus' temple bent.

Thus beauty's goddess caught what most she craved,

And her unconscious rival soon enslaved.

Cupid was there, and could no longer rest—

Trembling he clasped poor Psyche to his breast.
Propitious Jove thus eased his dire alarms,
And sent again the dear one to his arms.
Still locked together in a long embrace,
He looked into her eyes with pleading face,
Asking her forgiveness, and he confessed
That he had been too rash ; but now he vowed
He cared for her the more.   Her heart beat loud
Against her snowy bosom, and sadness
Yielded unto overpowering gladness.
E'en as a tender plant when dying sips
New vigour from a summer shower, her lips
All healthful grew, and unto Cupid bore
Such blissful essences, he doted more
Than he had ever done.   O truth is might !
For every punishment that Venus' spite
Invented to torment her captive fair,
She lightly bore, for now her whole despair
Was drowned in sudden happiness; but know
She could not from her dismal prison go.

The envy of the goddess 'gan t' abate,
And soon she proffered help instead of hate.
Venus no longer Cupid's favourite scorned,
But with new grace his paramour adorned.
She is immortal now, no more to sever
With Cupid, but to dwell with him for ever:
'Twas Constancy together kept the two,
Though parted, still unto each other true.

"Wilt thou so learn, my Daphnis, to be true?
And faithfulness as time rolls on renew?
O then what other lot could ours excel?
And what could be our harm who loved so well?
How pleasantly would seasons come and go!
Our new existence would be like the glow
Of morning's blush and setting sun's repose—
A sweet beginning and as sweet a close.
If thou dost love me tell it, and let's vow
In years to come to be as kind as now;
I think thou lovest me, still doubts do throng
About me, and I speak with greedy tongue,

3

For I would have thee all mine own to be
Part of myself, so would I be to thee."

Th' enraptured youth, as in her arms he lies,
Thus tremulous and faltering replies :
" Helen, if 'tis enchantment and I sleep,
O let my dream its present aspect keep !
Could I do otherwise than love thee ? nay,
Thou dost, sweet Helen, o'er my heart hold sway :
O may the power that hath drawn us nigh
Each other, keep us so until we die !
And dying bid us rise again to rove
Together in the palaces of Jove.
How glad to-morrow will the streamlets be
When I do sing to them in praise of thee ;
My flute will burst in music when it sips
The honey I have borrowed from thy lips.
All Cupid's cunningness, whate'er it be,
Could not outdo my fondness, dear, for thee ;
I vow by all the tender bonds of love
That Daphnis shall an honest suitor prove—

By ev'ry god that in the sky holds sway,
By ev'ry power that rules o'er night and day,
(Were I a god by awful Styx I'd vow
Even as I do by mine honour now)
By moon and stars that now upon us shine,
By our great Pan—and everything divine.
Helen, by what thou wilt—all things that are
In plains Elysian, earth, or brightest star."

And Helen thus : " My Daphnis, be it so,
Thus may our hearts together beat nor know
A change ; but rest invites us, and the rays
Of Jove's bright lamps illume the woodland ways.
The night seems all asleep, and every star
Twinkles in silence round Selene's car.
Everything is quiet—the sunless ground
Is wrapt up in a solitude profound."

Conversing thus they left the grotto's shade,
And down the mountains' moonlit footpaths strayed,

Until they came to where a pearly brook
Its way by little trees and bushes took.
Here rested they, when Helen slow began
In voice regretful and with visage wan :

" Now must we part alas ! for night is old,
And Helios soon will spread his wings of gold.
May calmest sleep fall gently o'er thine eyes,
Until the laughing daylight bids thee rise :
Or if thou dream may wingèd Morpheus shed
His poppy seeds of peace about thine head,
And scatter smoothly from his gilded horn,
Enchanting visions, till the burnished morn
Peeps o'er the hills ; and may thy mind's eye greet
The pleasantest of shapes, and may thy feet
Tread citron groves, and od'rous valleys where
The feath'ry halls of beauteous phantoms glare."

Another moment and the maid had flown,
And Daphnis all bewildered stood alone ;

In heavy dulness pining, where before
In solitude he mused, nor cared for more.
Then he pursued her : on he went and on,
Along the path where his beloved had gone.
Onward and onward still he wildly flew !
Though where he went or why he never knew ;
But jaded by despair to lose his mate,
He hurried on regardless of his fate,
Until the object of his chase he neared,
And 'twixt the boughs her graceful limbs appeared.

The amorous shepherd saw her join a band
Of naiads who were dancing hand in hand,
And paying tribute as their wont by night
With earnest songs unto their goddess bright.

As Daphnis drew unto the group more near,
Their invocations he could plainly hear :
In full solemnity their words arise,
To Venus, fairest goddess of the skies :

List ye trembling trees and flowers :
   All ye shining streams attend,
Whilst to Venus' sheeny bowers
   Our sweet harmonies ascend.
      As we pour
        Out her lays
      Evermore
        To her praise.
For it is our bounden duty
To the Queen of Love and Beauty
          Our song to raise.

All ye leafy woods and brakes
   Help us with a willing voice,
All ye bubbling rills and lakes
   Sing and evermore rejoice.
      Naiads sing,
        Play and prance,
      In a ring
        Let us dance.

Till the morning birds take wing,
And about our meadows sing,   .
   To Venus' praise
   Let us raise
A song until the valleys ring.
Lightly they sport, their slender forms nigh bare,
With smiling faces and dishevelled hair
That frolicked with the wind or fell to rest
On fairest shoulders or in fluttering breast.
A limpid brook went by, o'er which there grew
Clusters of drooping willow trees that threw
Their trembling branches down unto the flowers
About the brink, thus forming secret bowers,
Where these lithe creatures oft, with fretting heart,
Would from the rest in solitude depart,
And vent their sighs.   To such a hiding place
Did Daphnis his intruding footsteps trace ;
And there unseen between the boughs espied
The thoughtless group, and all their movements
  eyed.

As tiny fairy bands in moonshine play,
They tripped it o'er the lawn, and skipped away
To visit blobbing rills or forest's nook
Or bathe 'neath vines that overleap the brook,
Quickly they disappeared one by one.
He was alone again—Helen was gone!

The branches scarcely moved so still the night,
And yet he dare not go, dreading there might
Be some eye-witness in an ambush near
To scan his trick'ry, so did guilty fear
Encompass him; but see, ah! well-a-day!
He quakes and crouches back in blank dismay;
Not at ugly phantoms, but at a sight
Of loveliness. There was no time for flight,
For close from out a thicket straying slow,
In pensive mood, illumined with the glow
Of heaven's tapers, Echo came alone!
Sobbing and fretting in a woeful moan,
For dull Narcissus, slow and peevish boy—
Unlearned in maidens' charms and always coy.

With kisses and embraces many a dame
Had woo'd the lad to breed in him the flame
Of love, but all their practised arts were vain,
And he remained a simple silly swain.
Young Echo too had tried her many charms,
And pressed him in her round and snowy arms;
'Twas useless all, the dullard would not drink
From Cupid's cup, nor could he ever think
Why maidens cloyed his lips with every kiss
That chance allowed, and prate to him of bliss.
Poor Echo sighed unto the air her tale,
(Sick at heart) with many a low bewail.

    Echo denuded now unknowing shows
Herself to Daphnis—cause of many woes!
A sight forbidden, and unsought for too:
He looked and yet the danger well he knew.
Downcast she walked more slow, and meanwhile stayed
To sit beneath an oak tree's ample shade,
That faced the hidden youth. His very eyes
Made greedy feast upon this dainty prize:

This, Nature's finest work that drew its birth
From summer's musky breeze, and mother earth.
O when she prattled it was as the birds,
Or passing winds' soft lay tuned into words!
Had he been Narcissus for one short hour,
Or even had he been that precious flow'r
That lolled about her lap—how great a bliss
To be the branch that swayed adown to kiss
Her forehead, and to trifle with her hair!
For ever whispering, "daughter, most fair."
No longer could he gaze on grace so rare,
And be so near, yet linger idly there.
He settled every doubt, and with a spring,
He bounded forth to meet the precious thing.
Imploringly he muttered, "Maiden, fair!"
In great alarm she fled! as through the air
Re-echoed, "Maiden, fair-air-r."
                              Yet soon
All was as silent as the leering moon.
Stillness oft is fearful: now all around

Was beautifully calm, nor noise nor sound
Fell on his ear : 'twas as a sudden dream,
And startled, there he stood as he would seem
To doubt existence.   Slowly towards home
He in frightened steps began to roam,
Scarce daring to look round for very fear
That things e'en stranger he might see or hear.

From out their secret holes young rabbits came,
And frolicked round him in a merry game ;
The oak copse here and there they ran between,
And wildly chased each other o'er the green ;
They peeped at him from hedges in a way
That seemed to mock the lad, then ran away.
He walked until with dire affright he stayed,
And from the sky a voice unto him said :

" O, woe to thee who 'neath the cloak of night
Doth grope like some poor owl that dreads the light !
To pry into forbidden sights !—O hear !
A fate that thou can'st never shun, with fear !

Pure love with thee is all at end, and now
Inconstancy shall cheat thy truest vow;
Thy aims shall all be baffled, till thy breath
Leave thee a-gasping in the arms of death;
Existence shall be sour, and thou shalt crawl
In pain until thy fated end befall."

The voice was gone ! he staggered on his way,
And morning decked the clouds in garments grey.

PART III.

THUS did the naiad with dissembled charms,
With spicy accent and embracing arms,
O'ertake the lad, who vowed in that fond play,
By all the powers that rule o'er night and day,
To be a constant wooer, and ne'er own
Another's love, but hers, and hers alone.
Her smiles and well-used lips, and dreamy eyes
Too potent proved, and gained for her the prize.

Although the shepherd drooped, yet ne'er a word
He spoke of the dread voice that he had heard ;
But Helen soon, alas ! began to trace
Despondency in his lack-lustre face,
And he became less cheerful, for 'twas now
The fate foretold stamped sorrow on his brow.

One sunny noon as sitting in the shade
Upon a bank, fair Helen to him said :

" My Daphnis, prithee why art thou so dull ?
So strange to me ; thy very looks are full
Of woe : nay, do thou tell me of thy grief
That I may share it, and give thee relief.
Why dost thou gaze so fixedly ? now say
How fares thy flocks ?   Have any gone astray ?
Or fallen a prey ?   Alack ! all is not well.
Now, as thou lov'st me, all thy grievance tell ;
Have lambkins slipped the pent-up fold ? or say
Hath any hungry beast ta'en ought away ?"

 In answering, Daphnis was obliged to swerve
From truth, for nothing but a lie would serve ;
So thus he said : " As I do love thee well,
If I be sad, the cause I cannot tell.
'Tis but a change of mood ; we can't be gay
From morn to night, and smile throughout the day.
Pleasure is sweetest after pain, and so
All happiness is sweeter after woe—"

" Nay, do not dally with me," then she said,
" Nor look upon the ground ; lift up thy head,
Be cheerful as thou always wast till now ;
Be as thou used to be, and tell me how
This ranc'rous poison entered in thy heart ;
And how, and when, and wherefore came the
    smart."

" Had I calamities I would tell all
To thee," said Daphnis, " and how I did fall
To woefulness ; but Helen, I declare,
I have no secret pang, as thou art fair.
But I am drowsy now, and I would fain
Alone beneath these cooling boughs remain,
To sleep until this dulness may depart,
And give me once again a healthy heart."

Helen complies, and with a kiss she leaves,
She smiles on him, and yet for him she grieves.
    Alone once more, he sighs ; all round is glad,
Yet not with him, for he is wondrous sad ;

He brings to mind the voice that spake his end
Upon the night that he did most offend.
He sought not what he saw : that Echo strayed
Where he had seen her, or that naiads played
He cared not ; he only wished to see once more
His love, and part as sweetly as before.

A nymph saw Daphnis, and at once she ran
To where he sat, and craftily began
To woo him, but now deaf unto the strains
Of blabbing damsels, he unmoved remains.

"Dost thou not love?" quoth she, " O it were sad
For thou so comely and so fine a lad !"

He thus evades the nymph : " O yes ! I love
The beauties of the earth and sky above,
I love the outspread fields, I love the brooks,
I love all fern-grown solitary nooks,
I love to see our mountains, and I love
To watch the moon and myriad stars above ;

All pretty things and pure I love to see,
With lovely things and chaste I'd ever be."

About her eyes lurked glances that would tell,
Better than words, a meaning all too well;
But at her witching pranks and practised talk,
He feigns surprise, and skilfully doth balk
The nymph's endeavours.   So it is until
She speaks unto him even plainer still :

" Why look so sourly, boy ? am I not fair ?
Have I not rosy lips and flowing hair ?
Or would'st thou learn the softness of my breast,
Come, I will fondle thee, and thou mayst rest
Thy head upon my lap ; now what dost say ?
Wilt please thee if I go or if I stay ?"

His stubbornness she still contrives to cure,
And more and more, like Siren's song, doth lure.
Still he's unsavoury, so she tries again
To stop denial and to win the swain.

4

" Wilt be unruly like Narcissus boy ?
With power to bless, but aiming to annoy ;
And wilt thou, dearest, let me here remain
To woo like Echo, and to plead in vain ?
O no, it cannot be that one like thee
Should spurn a maiden and uncivil be !"
(As she the restless shepherd thus addressed,
She softly drew him nearer to her breast.)
" Nay, ponder on thy folly for awhile,"
(Then presses him still closer with a smile)
" Confess that thou dost like me ; not a word
By any but ourselves can here be heard."

Meanwhile Helen, who sad at heart had left,
Thinking that her own Daphnis peaceful slept,
Culls herbs from hedgerows and from thorny
        brakes,
The sleeper to refresh when he awakes.
And fruit she gathers ; then comes back again
Hoping to heal the suff'rer of his pain,

And round about his neck her arms to throw,
And on him all the fruit and herbs bestow.

Helen, too soon, alas ! the pair espied,
And sought behind the nearest tree to hide,
That she could overhear what they might say—
She curbs her passion yet can scarcely stay
Within her hiding-place.   Her face was flushed
With burning rage.   She could have madly rushed
Upon her prey, and played the tiger well,
For every nerve with fierce revenge did swell.
She hears a voice, "Now Daphnis I must leave,
But I until we meet again shall grieve.
Sure in thy absence all will go amiss ;
But farewell love," then followed kiss on kiss.
(A little trick in love will blight a life,
And in a moment cause eternal strife).

Soon as the nymph left Daphnis, Helen ran
Unto the lad, and vengeful thus began :
"O fiend most foul ! O cruel devil ! now
Where is thy truest love ? where is thy vow ?

May bitt'rest pangs gnaw ceaseless at thy heart,
And never may thy damnèd grief depart.
Deceiver most vile ! in misery grope,
Nor happiness regain, nor dream of hope.
Thou shalt be blind as worms—farewell ! farewell !
Both day and night shall be as black as hell !
Farewell ! enjoy thy new-love, now be sure
Farewell ! I'll interrupt thee never more."

    As she departed laughter rent the air,
And Daphnis sank to earth in blind despair.

PART IV.

ALL is very still, melancholy, dead ;
Every merry laugh from the plain is fled—
Goatherds sing no more, shepherds are not gay
Pan is sighing too, dryads will not play,
Flowers seem to droop, birds are wond'rous shy,
And wistfully do ask, " will Daphnis die ?"
The hare no longer leaps beside the hill :
All is hushed in silence ; mournful and still.
Little fishes rise in the stream and say,
" Doth sweet Daphnis still faint and die away ?"

In grief he shrank to nought — poor Daphnis
    pined ;
His coursers crouched about his feet and whined,
The jackals and the tigers mourned for him ;
The lions and the leopards grieved for him ;

For him all whispered one sad heavy lay
Of melancholy through the live-long day.

"O what a gloomy desert is the earth
Where cheerfulness is not, nor peace, nor mirth !"
Said Daphnis, who upon the ground had thrown
His weary limbs, and lingered all alone.
"When hope forsakes us, and when sullen care
Brings ne'er a vision but of blank despair.
When all is choked with pain, and eyes grow
     dim,
And life is cold and cloudy, and we swim
In troubled waters, panting for our breath,
Sick of all worldly things, yet fearing death.
What have I done that I such cruel hate
Should merit, and bring down so black a fate?
To wander in the dark, and never view
The many cherished scenes that once I knew,
Nor watch my lambkins frisk in simple play
Nor children sporting in the forest's way,

Passing a gladsome time before the morn
Of graver age with all its ills is born.

   Alack ! alack ! that I should thus be blind,
Without the power a moment's ease to find.
Sound is bereft of music without sight—
Fields cannot show their beauty without light.
On ev'ry side I hear a heavy swell
Of painful discord—one perpetual yell.

   No more may I look into that blue sky,
And see the cloudy phantoms passing by ;
Sailing in shapes fantastic, wild, and free,
On the blue ocean of eternity :
Unravelling their crystal rocks and peaks,
Flooded with light of many-coloured streaks,
And shining waters, too, so heavenly pure,
And forms too fanciful for words ; to lure
Affliction's sons and daughters to a spot
Beyond the stars, where troubles are forgot.
Such worlds of joy immutable there are
That far outshine our highest thoughts, ay far

That Jove foreshadows to his earthly born,
To give them patience in a world forlorn ;
Or why would man so crawl about the earth,
A thing of chance and misery from birth ?
Or who could 'neath a thousand sorrows bend
Whose soul did not foretell a peaceful end ?"

The shepherd ceased, and would have been at
    ease,
But cruel Venus came the lad to tease :
To taunt him tenderly, and add to pain
By speaking bitterly in smoothest strain.
Approaching thus she spake : " Why Daphnis, lad !
What ails thee now ? say why art thou so sad ?"
He answered not, whereat the goddess grew
Impatient, and nearer to Daphnis drew.
" Why art thou sitting here ? upon the hills
Where sunlight sparkles in the bounding rills,
Ardent swains in leafy bowers recline,
Wooing fair maids, whilst thou dost seek to pine !"

" I see thee not," he said, " but I can tell
That thou art Venus, for I know thee well.
If thou hast done in that most easing strain,
I pray thee still go on and rant again,
And gloat upon the wretched work thou'st wrought,
In dragging me from what I was to naught.
I know that thou did'st trace me everywhere,
And guided me with smiles into a snare :
Therefore I ask thee still again to prate,
It suits my mood and well befits my state.
When I did join the crazy host to pay
Tribute to thee, it was a cursèd day.
The sickly charm that round about thee lies,
Serves but to hide from unsuspectingeyes
Black vice enough to taint us all that dwell
Below the sky, and make another hell !
In thee are centred envy, lust, and hate,
Deceit and torment upon thee await ;
And even if pure passion from thee springs,
Then it is lost in all the ill it brings,

And turns from sweet to sour, until we fear
To look upon what once we held most dear,
I say thou art a devil clothed in light !
An evil vision beautiful to sight !
Thy lap full of fresh flowers thou dost bring,
But underneath a serpent lies to sting :
And as we take, it poisons our young blood,
Till we have nothing left within us good ;
Then our corrupted nature, sinking, feeds
On shame continual and wrongful deeds :
Falling degraded we grow all awry,
And writhe about like worms until we die."

   "Be not," she said, "so scornful with thy
      tongue,
For know that I have power to prolong
Thy torment, or to make it keener still ;
But I came not for that—'tis not my will,
Youth, even as I could make worse thy woe,
So I could make it lighter, and could throw

Vitality throughout, open thine eyes,
And show to thee again the hills and skies.
Thy troubles then would fade away and seem
No worse than is the mem'ry of a dream."

She ends her plea, whereat the shepherd sighs,
And turning to her angrily replies :
" Thou hast no power to help me if thou would'st,
Nor do I wish it even though thou could'st.
I am content to pine, and know thou this
That did'st thou paint a thousand scenes of bliss,
As I now am e'en would I so remain,
With ne'er a wish to tread the path again.
Rave till thou art hoarse, and then thou'lt find
No power to turn me from my present mind."
Baffled she leaves, and upward swiftly flies,
Steering her airy chariot through the skies.

The night came robed in sombre shrouds, and soon
Above the horizon peeped the yellow moon,

No noise was heard—tranquillity did fill
All things surrounding.   Daphnis lingered still.
  "Here," whispered he, "where crookèd oaks
    combine,
And sprawling branches round each other twine,
O let me die ! no longer would I stay—
My flutt'ring soul is ebbing fast away.
O Hermes ! who dost wait on our last breath,
To guide us to the mysteries after death.
O Father ! for 'twas so my mother said,
If thou art such, I now implore thy aid."

  He raised his head, and lo ! in radiance bright !
Clothed in the brilliancy of heavenly light,
Stood mighty Hermes, who advancing spoke,
At which the shepherd's slumbering soul awoke :
"Rest Daphnis, rest, all bitterness is o'er,
Now joy is thine, and peace for evermore."

THE END.

London :
J. C. Hotten, 74 and 75, Piccadilly.

RECENT POETRY.

A

CATALOGUE OF BOOKS

PUBLISHED BY

JOHN CAMDEN HOTTEN,

SWINBURNE'S POETICAL WORKS.

Foolscap 8vo., toned paper, cloth, price 3s. 6d.

SWINBURNE'S

SONG OF ITALY.

" Seldom has such a chant been heard, so full of glow, strength, and colour."—*Athenæum.*

SWINBURNE'S

POEMS AND BALLADS.

Fourth Edition, price 9s.

Demy 8vo., price 1s.

SWINBURNE'S

NOTES ON HIS POEMS,

AND ON THE REVIEWS WHICH HAVE APPEARED UPON THEM.

New Edition, foolscap 8vo., price 6s.

SWINBURNE'S

ATALANTA IN CALYDON.

LONDON: JOHN CAMDEN HOTTEN, 74 & 75, PICCADILLY.

SWINBURNE'S
CHASTELARD : A TRAGEDY.
New Edition, price 7s.

New Edition, foolscap 8vo., price 5s.

SWINBURNE'S
QUEEN MOTHER, AND ROSAMOND.

In Preparation.

SWINBURNE'S
BOTHWELL.
A NEW POEM.

THE POCKET SHELLEY.

*Uniform with the Tauchnitz Series, in Illustrated Wrapper, price 1s. 8d. ;
or cloth elegant, 2s. 2d.*

THE POETICAL WORKS OF PERCY BYSSHE SHELLEY.
From the Author's Original Editions.

FIRST SERIES: QUEEN MAB, AND THE EARLY POEMS.

" A very charming edition of a charming poet."—*Standard.*
" It may be doubted whether any editions, not excluding the now cele-
brated edition of Mr. W. M. Rossetti, will be greater favourites with the
students of the poet than these curious volumes. Now for the first time we
have an exact reprint of the *Queen Mab* and early poems, in the form in
which they were given by the poet to the world."—*Sunday Times.*

OLD DRAMATISTS—NEW EDITIONS.

Crown 8vo., Portrait, cloth, 6s. ; cloth gilt, 6s. 6d.

MARLOWE'S (CHRISTOPHER) WORKS ;
Including his Translations. Edited, with Notes and Introduction, by
Lieut.-Col. F. CUNNINGHAM.

Crown 8vo., Portrait, cloth, 6s.; cloth gilt, 6s. 6d.

MASSINGER'S (PHILIP) PLAYS.
From the Text of WM. GIFFORD. With the addition of the Tragedy of
" Believe as You List." Edited by Lieut.-Col. FRANCIS CUNNINGHAM.

LONDON: JOHN CAMDEN HOTTEN, 74 & 75, PICCADILLY.

Complete in 3 vols., crown 8vo., Portrait, cloth, 6s. each; cloth gilt, 6s. 6d. each.

BEN JONSON'S WORKS.

With Notes Critical and Explanatory, and a Biographical Memoir, by WILLIAM GIFFORD. Edited by Lieut.-Col. FRANCIS CUNNINGHAM.

Foolscap 8vo., cloth neat, bevelled boards, price 3s. 6d.

KITTY CRUMP:

A ROMANCE OF LOVE'S YOUNG DREAM, AND OTHER POEMS.

By FREDERICK LANGBRIDGE.

"The poems are decidedly creditable to so young a poet."—*Echo.*

"There is a pleasant vein of humour in several of the pieces, and a quaint touch or two of that antithesis which was such a charm in Praed's poems." *Birmingham Daily Post.*

"The play of the humour is genuine and unaffected, and the story is really well told."—*Birmingham Daily Gazette.*

A cheap edition, in paper covers, is also published, price 1s.

BRET HARTE'S POEMS.

Foolscap 8vo., Illustrated Wrapper, price 1s.; or fine edition, crown 8vo., with " That Heathen Chinee" set to Music by STEPHEN TUCKER, *and humorous illustrations, price 3s. 6d.*

THAT HEATHEN CHINEE,

AND OTHER HUMOROUS POEMS.

By BRET HARTE.

"Mr. Bret Harte's poems, serious as well as humorous, are such as to tempt the reader not to lay aside this volume until he has finished it."—*Kelso Courier.*

By the same Author, foolscap 8vo., Illustrated Wrapper, price 1s.; or cloth neat, bevelled boards, 2s. 6d.

EAST AND WEST: SKETCHES IN VERSE.

"Mr. Bret Harte seems to be taking a foremost place among trans atlantic poets, and *East and West* is in some respects the best thing he ha done. The comic parts are equal to *Bon Gaultier*."—*Graphic.*

'The simple and touching beauty of the first little piece in this collection ['A Greyport Legend'] will prepossess the reader in favour of the whole. Longfellow might have written such a poem, and been proud of it."—*News of the World.*

LONDON: JOHN CAMDEN HOTTEN, 74 & 75, PICCADILLY

CHOICEST HUMOROUS POETRY OF THE AGE.

Foolscap 8vo., Illustrated Wrapper, price 1s.; or fine edition, with coloured illustrations by GEORGE CRUIKSHANK, *3s. 6d.*

THE BIGLOW PAPERS.

BY J. RUSSELL LOWELL.

With Notes, Glossary, and Introduction. The best and fullest edition of these Humorous and very Clever Verses.

Foolscap 8vo., 450 pages, fine Portrait and Autograph, 7s. 6d.; uniform with MR. SWINBURNE'S *Poems.*

WALT WHITMAN'S POEMS.

(LEAVES OF GRASS, DRUM-TAPS, &c.)

Selected and edited by WILLIAM MICHAEL ROSSETTI.

"Whitman is a poet who bears and needs to be read as a whole, and then the volume and torrent of his power carry the disfigurements along with it and away.—He is really a fine fellow."—*Chambers's Journal.*

Small 4to., elegantly printed on toned paper, full gilt, gilt edges, for the Drawing-room, price 6s.

CAROLS OF COCKAYNE.

BY HENRY S. LEIGH.

Vers de Société, and charming Verses descriptive of London Life. With numerous exquisite little designs by ALFRED CONCANEN.

Foolscap 8vo., cloth neat, price 4s. 6d.

ODD ECHOES FROM OXFORD.

BY A. MERION, B.A.

A POETICAL SATIRE.

Crown 8vo., price 3s. 6d.

HORSE & FOOT; OR, PILGRIMS TO PARNASSUS.

BY RICHARD CRAWLEY.

"I'll not march through Coventry with them, that's flat."

"Whatever may be thought of this spirited satire of 841 lines, no one will accuse its writer of personality; and however hard he may hit some of the literati of the day, he appears to write in perfect good faith, and, in thus frankly avowing his own critical convictions, to be influenced but by one thought—the healthy interests of English literature. Without acquaintance with those mentioned in his pages, 'or indeed with any one in the literary world,' Mr. Crawley writes 'independently,' and for this moral courage we thank him."

LONDON: JOHN CAMDEN HOTTEN, 74 & 75, PICCADILLY.

COMPANION TO "BON GAULTIER BALLADS."

Small 4to., printed within an India-paper tone, elegantly bound, gilt edges, price 10s. 6d.

PUCK ON PEGASUS.

By H. CHOLMONDELEY PENNELL.

This most amusing work has already passed through Six Editions, receiving everywhere the highest praise as "a clever and brilliant book." To no other work of the present day have so many distinguished Artists contributed Illustrations. In addition to the designs of GEORGE CRUIKSHANK, JOHN LEECH, JULIAN PORTCH, "PHIZ," and other Artists, Sir NOEL PATON, MILLAIS, JOHN TENNIEL, RICHARD DOYLE, and M. ELLEN EDWARDS, have now contributed several exquisite pictures, thus making the New Edition —which is twice the size of the old one, and contains irresistibly funny pieces—the best book for the Drawing-room table published.

"The epigrammatic drollery of Mr. Cholmondeley Pennell's ' Puck on Pegasus ' is well known to many of our readers. . . . The present is a superb and handsomely printed and illustrated edition of this book."—*Times.*

"A beautiful and amusing book. The illustrations are all more or less charming."—*Scotsman.*

"Who does not know ' Puck on Pegasus,' which now comes before us in a sixth edition ?"—*London Review.*

" . . . . Splendid verse. The sixth edition —on the merits of the book it ought to be the sixtieth—is published in exquisite garb by Mr. Hotten. Those who do not already know the wonderful swing of Mr. Cholmondeley Pennell's lines should make their acquaintance at once. ' Jolly ' is hardly the word for the book, either in the writing or the get up, but we make ' Puck on Pegasus ' a present of it, for want of a better."—*Standard.*

By the same Author, crown 8vo., elegantly printed and bound, price 6s.

MODERN BABYLON,
AND OTHER POEMS.

Uniform with the Tauchnitz Series, in Illustrated Wrapper, price 1s ; or cloth elegant, price 1s. 6d.

HOOD'S WHIMS AND ODDITIES.
Both Series complete, with 80 Illustrations.

Crown 8vo, toned paper, elegant, price 3s. 6d.

WIT & HUMOUR.
By the "AUTOCRAT OF THE BREAKFAST TABLE."

A volume of delightfully humorous Poems, very similar to the mirthful verses of Tom Hood.

A cheap edition is also published, in foolscap 8vo., Illustrated Wrapper, price 1s.

LONDON : JOHN CAMDEN HOTTEN, 74 & 75, PICCADILLY.

Uniform with the Tauchnitz Series, in Illustrated Wrapper, price 1s.; in cloth, 1s. 6d.

HANS BREITMANN'S BALLADS.

THE COMPLETE WORK.

From the Author's Revised Copyright.

I.—Hans Breitmann's Party.   II.—Hans Breitmann's Christmas.
III.—Hans Breitmann's Velocipede.   IV.—Hans Breitmann's Der
Freyschutz.   V.—Hans Breitmann's other Ballads.

"PIKE COUNTY BALLADS."

Foolscap 8vo., Illustrated Wrappers, price 1s.; or cloth neat, bevelled boards, 2s. 6d.

LITTLE BREECHES, AND OTHER PIECES.

By COLONEL JOHN HAY.

"We soon discover real genius in the book, that indescribable radiance that distinguishes true poetry from mere versification.   Colonel Hay is a poet of whom America ought to be proud."—*Public Opinion.*
"The most original verses we have read for some time.   Some of the short poems are exquisite."—*Lloyd's News.*

Square 8vo., Illustrated Wrapper, price 1s.; or in cloth, price 2s. 6d., beautifully printed.

POLICEMAN Y: HIS OPINIONS ON WAR AND THE MILLINGTARY.

By JOHN E. SODEN.

With Illustrations by the Author.

** Readers of Thackeray's "Policeman X Ballads" will be much amused with the "Opinions" of his brother officer, "Policeman Y."
"Amusing these ballads certainly are; and the illustrations are very characteristic."—*Lloyd's Weekly Paper.*
"A book we can strongly recommend."—*Echo.*

Now ready, foolscap 8vo., cloth neat, price 4s. 6d., a Second Edition of

FOOTPRINTS: POEMS TRANSLATED AND ORIGINAL.

By GEORGE BROWNING.

"Mr. Browning has many gentle and poetical thoughts.   The original poems seem largely influenced by the German studies of the writer."—*Sunday Times.*
"There is the ring of true poetry in his lines; he is throughout so thoroughly in earnest, that we gladly welcome him as a worthy recruit to the small band of minor poets of the present day."—*Court Circular.*
"Mr. George Browning's little collection of original and translated lyrical pieces displays much genuine poetical feeling and fancy."—*Figaro.*

LONDON: JOHN CAMDEN HOTTEN, 74 & 75, PICCADILLY.

A TRUE PICTURE OF THE MODERN FASHIONABLE WORLD.

Elegantly bound for the Drawing-room, price 5s., by post 5s. 4d.

THE SEASON : A SATIRE.

By ALFRED AUSTIN.

An entirely New Edition of the famous Work.

"Mr. Austin has the heart of a true poet. the brain of a shrewd thinker, and the pen of an accomplished writer."—*Dublin University Magazine.*

"The best verses of their kind since 'English Bards and Scotch Reviewers.'"—*The Queen's Messenger.*

"One of the most powerful satires of modern times."—*Daily News.*

"Mr. Austin's splendid talents as a satirist are beyond all question." —*The Era.*

"We venture to welcome the birth of another poet among us in Mr. Austin, and we bid him hearty speed."—*London Review.*

"Keen, glittering. pungent, and clever."—*Weekly Dispatch.*

"Has not been surpassed since Byron's days."—*Illustrated Times.*

Crown 8vo., with Frontispiece, 500 pp., 7s. 6d.

GEORGE COLMAN'S BROAD GRINS:

MY NIGHTGOWN AND SLIPPERS, and other Humorous Works, Prose and Poetical, of GEORGE COLMAN, the Younger.

Now first collected, with Life and Anecdotes of the Author,

By GEORGE B. BUCKSTONE.

Admirers of genuine old English wit and humour—irresistible and always fresh—will be delighted with the collected edition of George Colman's humorous works. As a wit, he has had no equal in our time.

In green and gold, 5s. 6d.

INFELICIA.

POEMS BY ADAH ISAACS MENKEN.

Illustrated with NUMEROUS GRACEFULLY PENCILLED DESIGNS DRAWN ON WOOD BY ALFRED CONCANEN. Dedicated, by permission, to CHARLES DICKENS, with photographic facsimile of his letter, and a very beautifully engraved portrait of the Authoress.

"It is full of pathos and sentiment, displays a keen appreciation of beauty, and has remarkable earnestness and passion."—*Globe.*

"A loving and delicate care has been bestowed on perhaps the daintiest pages of verse that have been issued for many years."—*Lloyd's News.*

"Few, if any, could have guessed the power and beauty of the thoughts that possessed her soul, and found expression in language at once pure and melodious. . . . . Who shall say Menken was not a poet? Throughout her verse there runs a golden thread of rich and pure poetry."—*Press.*

"There is a passionate richness about many of the poems which is almost startling."—*Sunday Times.*

"An amazing little book, unhappily posthumous, which a distinguished woman has left as a legacy to mankind and the ages."—*Saturday Review.*

LONDON: JOHN CAMDEN HOTTEN, 74 & 75, PICCADILLY.

A FEW COPIES ONLY ISSUED FOR ADMIRERS OF THE POET.
Royal 16mo, beautifully bound in green and gold, price 4s. 6d.

JOAQUIN, ET AL.

By CINCINNATUS H. MILLER.

(From the Edition published in Oregon.)

The original volume of poems published by Joaquin Miller, author of "Songs of the Sierras." The first drafts of some of his finest poems will be found here, together with several compositions altogether new to English readers.

Crown 8vo., cloth, with the whole of ROWLANDSON'S *Illustrations, in colours, after the original drawings, price 7s. 6d.*

DR. SYNTAX'S THREE TOURS

IN SEARCH OF THE PICTURESQUE, OF CONSOLATION, AND OF A WIFE.

The Three Series Complete, with a Life of this industrious Author—the English Le Sage—now first written by JOHN CAMDEN HOTTEN.

One of the most amusing and laughable books ever published.

In crown 8vo., cloth, price 3s. 6d.

THE PROMETHEUS BOUND OF ÆSCHYLUS.

Translated in the Original Metres by C. B. CAYLEY, B.A.

"This new translation will, we doubt not, be warmly welcomed as ably carrying out the object which the writer seeks to achieve—that of familiarising English readers, through the medium of their own language, with the stately forms and the scientific principles of the Greek versification. In this, as well as in preserving the spirit of the original, the writer has eminently succeeded."—*Observer.*

Foolscap 8vo., elegantly bound, price 3s. 6d.

GRAZIELLA ; OR, MY FIRST SORROW,

AND OTHER POEMS.

By A. DE LAMARTINE.

The original French ; with a translation into English verse

By WALTER CHARLES URQUHART.

"To translate Lamartine's poetry requires talents of no mean order, and we may congratulate Mr. Urquhart upon having passed through the ordeal successfully."—*Liverpool Leader.*

LONDON: JOHN CAMDEN HOTTEN, 74 & 75, PICCADILLY.

12mo., same size as Tennyson's " MAUD," price 5s.

TRANSLATIONS FROM CHARLES BAUDELAIRE,

With a few ORIGINAL POEMS, by R. H. SHEPHERD.

Bound in vellum cloth and Etruscan gold, a most beautiful and captivating volume, price 12s. 6d.

ANACREON (Moore's Translation).

Illustrated by the exquisite Designs of GIRODET.

The well-known Paris house, Firmin Didot, a few years since produced a miniature edition of these exquisite designs by the photographic process, and sold a large number at £2 per copy. The designs have been universally admired by both artists and poets.

Now ready, a choice little volume, price 4s.

ANACREON IN ENGLISH:

Attempted in the Metres of the Original.

By THOMAS J. ARNOLD.

Crown 8vo., cloth extra, price 7s. 6d., a volume of

CHINESE BALLADS AND POEMS IN ENGLISH VERSE.

UNDER THE PEAK;

JOTTINGS IN VERSE DURING A RESIDENCE IN HONG KONG.

By W. T. MERCER, M.A.

Containing, with many other Poems, the following :—
A String of Hong Kong Sonnets. Ode to the Sons of Han. Chinese Vers de Société. Keyang's Farewell. The Man of Loo. The Hanyang Thistle. Chaou Yung's Quatrain. Trifles from the Tartar. Taifoong. The Sun of Hong Kong. The Tea Ballad. &c., &c.

Crown 8vo., Illustrated Wrapper, price 6d.

THE DRAMA ON CRUTCHES.

A SATIRE OF THE DAY.

By W. R. SNOW.

By the same Author, square 8vo., price 6d., with an Illustration.

BRITANNIA'S BOX OF SOLDIERS.

LONDON: JOHN CAMDEN HOTTEN, 74 & 75, PICCADILLY.

Crown 8vo., handsomely printed, price 1s.,

WITH ILLUSTRATIONS BY ERNEST GRISET,

THE HUSBAND AND WIFE WHO NEVER QUARRELLED.

BY A BACHELOR.

New Edition, beautifully Illustrated, cloth elegant, royal 8vo., price 6s.

THE VALE OF LANHERNE,

AND OTHER CORNISH POEMS.

BY HENRY SEWELL STOKES.

Illustrated with Eight beautiful Tinted Lithographs of the following most picturesque spots in Cornwall:—THE VALE OF LANHERNE, THE NUNNERY OF LANHERNE, THE CHURCH OF ST. MAWGAN, ANCIENT CROSS OF MAWGAN, and Views of the Sea Coast, including FALLORY, TREGURRION BAY, THE NORWEGIAN'S ROCK, THE EYRY, &c.

"The work, from its intrinsic merits, is worthy of a wide circulation, and will be read with pleasure by all lovers of thoughtful and melodious verse."—*Tait's Magazine.*

By the same Author, foolscap 8vo., cloth, with Photograph of the Land's End, a pretty volume, price 6s. 6d.

RHYMES FROM CORNWALL.

"Any one who proposes to take a walking tour through Cornwall, will do well to put this little book in his knapsack on setting out."—*Irish Times.*

Square 8vo., cloth gilt, price 7s. 6d.

RECREATIONS AT MAGDALA.

BY CAPTAIN CAMERON,

Late H.B.M. Consul at Massowah.

Crown 8vo., printed Wrapper, price 6d.

EPISTLE TO THE DEIL.

BY HOLY WILLIE OF PRUSSIA.

Square 8vo., cloth, price 5s.

PAUL: A TRAGEDY OF GLAMOUR.

IN FIVE ACTS.

"The author has thrown into a poetical form what is a real history, and constitutes, indeed, the characteristic tragedy of the Church."

LONDON: JOHN CAMDEN HOTTEN, 74 & 75, PICCADILLY.

Now ready, a handsome volume, foolscap 8vo., price 6s.

FAIR ROSAMOND, AND OTHER POEMS.

BY B. MONTGOMERIE RANKING (of the Inner Temple).

"The declamation of Rizpah by the bodies of her sons is given with considerable vigour and natural feeling. . . . Contains much unusually valuable poetry, with nothing that will not repay the reader who can enjoy many and varied themes diversely treated."—*Athenæum.*
"There are a number of very pretty sonnets, for which the author deserves a high compliment."—*Sun.*

By the same Author, uniform, price 4s. 6d.

POEMS.

Square 8vo., cloth, price 7s. 6d.

FLYING CHILDERS—HIS CRUISE.

BY THE EARL OF WINCHILSEA.

An elegant little volume, bound in blue and gold, carmine edges, price 4s. 6d.

LYRICS AND BUCOLICS.

The Eclogues of Virgil, a Selection from the Odes of Horace, and the Legend of the Sibyl.

Translated by HERBERT NOYES.

"There is a certain freedom and swing in these translations, which not only more resembles the brisk spirit and ringing tone of the original, but is truly refreshing after the stiff rendering which had been generally made of Horace's choicest composition. We become grateful for new renderings, which, whilst they retain as much of the spirit and force of the original as translations can, vehicle the old Roman thoughts through sweet measures, and dainty rhythmic melodies."—*London Review.*

By the same Author, in uniform binding, price 9s.

AN IDYLL' OF THE WEALD.

WITH OTHER LAYS AND LEGENDS.

Foolscap 8vo., cloth neat, price 5s.

POEMS FROM THE GREEK MYTHOLOGY;

AND MISCELLANEOUS POEMS.

BY EDMUND OLLIER.

"What he has written is enough, and more than enough, to give him a high rank amongst the most successful cultivators of the English Muse."—*Globe.*

LONDON: JOHN CAMDEN HOTTEN, 74 & 75, PICCADILLY.

Crown 8vo., handsomely printed, price 6s.

THE IDOLATRESS ; AND OTHER POEMS.

By DR. JAMES WILLS,

Author of "Dramatic Scenes," "The Disembodied," &c.

"One great merit of the 'Idolatress' is to be found in the ability with which the writer has contrasted a spiritual faith and its claims on the conscience, with a material faith that captivates the imagination through the senses."—*Athenæum.*

Foolscap 8vo., cloth neat, price 5s.

ADELINE.   A POEM IN SEVEN CANTOS.

By J. HECTOR COURCELLE.

Foolscap 8vo., cloth neat, price 2s. 6d.

FACTS AND FANCIES FROM THE FARM.

POEMS BY JAMES DAWSON.

"Here we have some very pretty and readable poems—some of it so much above the average as to warrant expectations of something far better, and we shall look forward with interest to the next volume from the same hand."—*Globe.*

A Cheap Edition is also published, in paper covers, price 1s.

Square 12mo., cloth, bevelled boards, price 6s.

UNDER DEAD LEAVES;

AND OTHER POEMS.

By W. E. WINDUS.

Crown 8vo , three handsome volumes, price 7s. 6d. each.

POEMS AND SONNETS,

PARTS I., II., AND III.

By GEORGE BARLOW, Ex. Coll. Oxon.

"There are grace and melody in the pieces entitled 'Reminiscence and 'The Discovery of Love,' and another called 'The Waking of Beauty' shows a genuine worship, which ought some time to bear worthier fruit."—*Spectator.*

"A new singer to us is Mr. Barlow, but one who unquestionably fingers the chords of his harp with a somewhat masterly touch ; . . . owning, apparently, within himself, inexhaustible resources of heart-melody."—*Public Opinion.*

Speaking of Part I., the *Illustrated News* says :—"The first part only of a collection which, thus far, reveals so many graces, that a reader of taste may well wait impatiently for the second."

"The volume has a fine human sentiment of its own. There is a sympathy with nature which is not accepted at second hand, but which bursts forth from the inner personality of the writer."—*Weekly Dispatch.*

LONDON: JOHN CAMDEN HOTTEN, 74 & 75, PICCADILLY.

Foolscap 8vo., handsomely bound, price 5s.

TIMOTHY COTTON;

CANTOS I. TO III.

With a Dedication to the Shade of Don Juan.

Just out, foolscap 8vo., with wood-cuts, cloth, very neat, price 6s.

AN EPIC OF WOMEN,

AND OTHER POEMS.

By ARTHUR W. E. O'SHAUGHNESSY.

With some Original Designs by Mr. J. T. NETTLESHIP.

"What he has given us is remarkable. With its quaint title, and quaint illustrations, 'An Epic of Women' will be a rich treat to a wide circle of admirers."—*Athenæum.*

"Combine Morris and Swinburne, and inspire the product with a fervour essentially original, and you have, as we take it, a fair notion of Mr. O'Shaughnessy's poems."—*Dispatch.*

4to., toned paper, very elegant, price 10s. 6d.

BIANCA: POEMS AND BALLADS.

By EDWARD BRENNAN.

By the same Author, foolscap 8vo., cloth neat, price 6s.

AMBROSIA AMORIS.

Foolscap 8vo., price 7s. 6d.

STRAWBERRY HILL;

AND OTHER POEMS.

By COLBURN MAYNE, ESQ.

"It is a bright, clever little book, in which we find a great deal of good rhyme, and some genuine and pleasing poetry. There are several charming pictures of the historic group which we know from Horace Walpole's letters and Sir Joshua's paintings."—*Morning Star.*

Foolscap 8vo., elegantly printed, price 3s. 6d.

THE VILLAGE ON THE FORTH;

AND OTHER POEMS.

By PHILIP LATIMER.

LONDON: JOHN CAMDEN HOTTEN, 74 & 75, PICCADILLY.

OLD ENGLISH RELIGIOUS BALLADS AND CAROLS.
Small 4to., with beautiful floriated borders, Renaissance style, cloth gilt, price 12s. 6d.

SONGS OF THE NATIVITY.

An entirely new collection of Old Carols, including some never before given in any collection. With Music to the more popular.
Edited by W. H. HUSK.
Librarian to the Sacred Harmonic Society.

Foolscap 8vo., Printed Wrapper, price 2s. 6d.

A HUNDRED SONNETS.

By JOHN C. EARLE, B.A. Oxon., Author of "English Premiers."

By the same Author, Foolscap 8vo., cloth, price 3s. 6d.

A SECOND HUNDRED SONNETS.

In foolscap 8vo., price 4s. 6d.

NEW AND OLD:

A MORNING REVERIE,
Commemorative of the Political and Ecclesiastical Crisis of 1867—8.
By D. McIVOR,
Author of "The Wanderer," "Fantasia, a Vision."
"'New and Old' undoubtedly gives evidence of the possession of considerable poetic talent and high culture."—*Press.*

Foolscap 8vo., cloth, 5s.; half-morocco, 6s.

ECHOES FROM THE FRENCH POETS.

An Anthology from BAUDELAIRE, ALFRED DE MUSSET, LAMARTINE, VICTOR HUGO, A. CHENIER, T. GAUTIER, BERANGER, NADAUD, DUPONT, PARNY, and others.
By HARRY CURWEN.
"A short poem of Théophile Gautier's Mr. Curwen has really put before the English public in the most welcome manner. The 'Spectre of the Rose.' is unexceptionable."—*Lloyd's News.*
"A pleasant little volume of translations from modern French poets."—*Graphic.*

In crown 8vo., cloth elegant, price 6s.

SO FAR.

By HERBERT RANDOLPH.

LONDON: JOHN CAMDEN HOTTEN, 74 & 75, PICCADILLY.

Square 8vo., cloth, price 4s. 6d.

WAYSIDE SKETCHES,

IN PROSE AND VERSE.

By EDWARD LEGGE.

" These are agreeable little pieces in prose and verse. . . . Many of the verses are sweetly and tunefully written."—*Era.*

Foolscap 8vo., cloth, price 2s. 6d.

SCRAPS OF VERSE.

By THE LATE REV. N. OR M.

Foolscap 8vo., very neat, price 2s. 6d.

THE ESTABLISHMENT;

OR, THE CHURCH IN DANGER : A SATIRE.

By AN ARCHDEACON.

" We recommend those who have the welfare of the Church at heart to read this rhymed satire, in which they will find both reason and right."—*Public Opinion.*

Foolscap 8vo., cloth, price 3s. 6d.

DAPHNIS THE UNFAITHFUL :

A POETIC ROMANCE.

By GUY ROSLYN, A MINOR.

" Is evidently written by one who is ardently attached to mythology."—*The Echo.*

" This is a pretty little pastoral poem, creditable to the ability and taste of the author, and giving promise of future excellence."—*News of the World.*

" The author of this poem sings of the loves of the immortals—their jealousy and their constancy. * * * If Mr. Roslyn be what he is described on the title-page, a minor, we may well congratulate him on the success of this effort of his genius, as giving good promise for the future which we trust to see realised at no distant date."—*Era.*

In very elegant gilt binding, price 6s.

BRITANNIA AND COLUMBIA;

AND OTHER POEMS.

By HESPER HATTERAS.

" Mr. Hatteras writes well, and his poetry, which flows with remarkable smoothness, is studded with the most graceful of imagery, whilst it shows a depth of feeling which will be sure to make him popular."—*Era.*

LONDON: JOHN CAMDEN HOTTEN, 74 & 75, PICCADILLY.

Crown 8vo., very elegant, price 7s. 6d.

LYRICAL RECREATIONS.

By SAMUEL WARD.

" Lyrics written in a lively, cheerful spirit ; all evidencing good feeling, many of them graceful in design and tastefully worded."—*Public Opinion.*

Foolscap 8vo., cloth, very neat, price 3s. 6d.

LIGHTS AND SHADOWS ; AND OTHER POEMS.

By JOHN R. BLACKFORD.

Crown 8vo., green cloth, bevelled boards, price 3s. 6d.

PHÆDRA ; AND OTHER POEMS.

By HENRY MARTIN.

Oblong 4to, prettily bound, price 4s. 6d., with steel plate frontispiece,

EMMABURG:

A LEGEND IN VERSE, IN FOUR CANTOS.,
BY THE HON. ROGER G. MOLYNEUX.

Crown 8vo., cloth, price 3s. 6d.

MUSINGS IN VERSE.

By N. M.

12mo., gilt cloth, gilt edges, 3s.

ACROSTICS, IN PROSE AND VERSE.

Edited by A. E. H.

Also Published,

A SECOND SERIES, cloth gilt, 3s.
A THIRD SERIES, cloth gilt, 3s.
A FOURTH SERIES. With 8 Pictorial Acrostics. Cloth gilt, 3s.
A FIFTH SERIES. An entirely Original Work. Cloth gilt, 4s. 6d.
A SUPPLEMENT, under the title of " Easy Double, Historical, and Scriptural Acrostics." Cloth gilt, 3s.

The volumes comprise Single, Double, Treble, and every variety of Acrostics.—Each Series sold separately ; or the Five Series complete in a Case, "THE ACROSTIC BOX," price 15s.

LONDON: JOHN CAMDEN HOTTEN, 74 & 75, PICCADILLY.

10